Hello, Baby Mo!

EMMA SHEVAH

ILLUSTRATED BY KATIE SAUNDERS

BLOOMSBURY EDUCATION

LONDON   OXFORD   NEW YORK   NEW DELHI   SYDNEY

BLOOMSBURY EDUCATION
Bloomsbury Publishing Plc
50 Bedford Square, London, WC1B 3DP, UK

BLOOMSBURY, BLOOMSBURY EDUCATION and the Diana logo
are trademarks of Bloomsbury Publishing Plc

First published in Great Britain 2019 by Bloomsbury Publishing Plc

A catalogue record for this book is available from the British Library

ISBN: PB: 978-1-4729-6346-8; ePDF: 978-1-4729-6347-5; ePub: 978-1-4729-6348-2;
enhanced ePub: 978-1-4729-6959-0

2 4 6 8 10 9 7 5 3 1

Printed and bound in China by Leo Paper Products, Heshan, Guangdong

MIX
Paper from
responsible sources
FSC® C020056

All papers used by Bloomsbury Publishing Plc are natural, recyclable products
from wood grown in well managed forests. The manufacturing processes conform
to the environmental regulations of the country of origin

To find out more about our authors and books visit www.bloomsbury.com
and sign up for our newsletters

Chapter One

Adam came home with a new book. The same day, his mum came home with a new baby.

"I've gone up a reading level. Look, I've got a new book!" Adam cried.

"We've got something new, too," Mum
said. "Look." She bent down so Adam
could see.
Adam looked at the tiny, red face.
The baby's eyes were closed.
"Is he my brother?"
Adam asked.

"She's your sister," Dad replied. "She's called Mo. Isn't she lovely?"

Adam didn't think she was lovely. He
wanted a brother. His house was full of
new stuff and it was all for the baby.
And he didn't like the name Mo.
Adam liked his new book, though.
"Let's read it!" he said.

"Later, Adam," Mum said. "Mo's hungry and so are we."
Mum put Mo down and Dad started to cook dinner.
"**Waaaaaahhhh!**" cried Mo.

Chapter Two

But they didn't read Adam's book later. Mo cried all evening. Mum rocked her. Dad rocked her. But nothing helped.

Waaaaaahhhh!

Waaaaaahhhh!

Waaaaaaahhhh!

Mo was still crying when
Adam went to sleep.

The next morning, Dad was so tired that he spread butter on Adam's toast. Adam didn't like butter on his toast. Dad made Adam a cup of tea. Adam didn't drink tea. Then Dad put the kettle in the fridge.

"Dad?" Adam asked. "Are you OK?"
"Hmm?" Dad asked. His hair was
sticking up and he looked confused.
"Never mind," Adam muttered. "Can
we read my book now?"

"Sure," Dad replied. He sat next to Adam and rested his head on his arms. "Once there was…" Adam began. But Dad had fallen asleep.

Mum was changing Mo's nappy again.
"Can we read now?" Adam asked.
"Soon," Mum said. "Where's Dad?"
"Asleep," Adam said.
"Go and wake him," Mum said. "We
need more nappies."

"**Waaaaaahhhh!**" cried Mo.

Chapter Three

Adam woke Dad up. It wasn't easy.

Dad went to the corner shop and Mum sat down to feed Mo.
Adam sat beside Mum with his book in his hand. He didn't like this baby.

Everything was fine before she arrived.
Now Mum and Dad were always busy
and tired. And no one wanted to hear
him read. He had gone up a level but he
hadn't even read his new book yet!

Dad came home with nappies. He rubbed
his eyes and said, "I need a shower.
Back soon."

"Look Adam," Mum whispered. "She's
asleep. At last! I'll put her in her basket."

"Good," Adam growled. "Can we read my book now?"

"Oh, Adam! Mo kept me awake all night. I need to lie down. Just for a few minutes," Mum said.

"We'll read it as soon as I wake up.
I promise."
And she lay on the sofa with a
groan.

Chapter Four

Adam was angry. When was he going to read his new book? And how could this tiny baby be so much trouble?

"Eeeeeh!" squealed Mo. She had woken up!

Adam stood over her basket. Mo wriggled and made funny faces, which made Adam smile. Then Mo made more noises. Unhappy noises. Was she going to cry again?

"Mum?" Adam whispered. But Mum was asleep.

"Dad?" Adam called. But Dad was in the shower.

Adam didn't know what to do. He picked up a toy rattle and waved it in front of Mo. Suddenly, Mo stopped crying.

Adam held Mo's tiny fingers and said,
"Hello. Why do you cry so much? Can't
you see I have a new book to read?"
Mo gripped Adam's finger with her
little hand. Adam smiled.

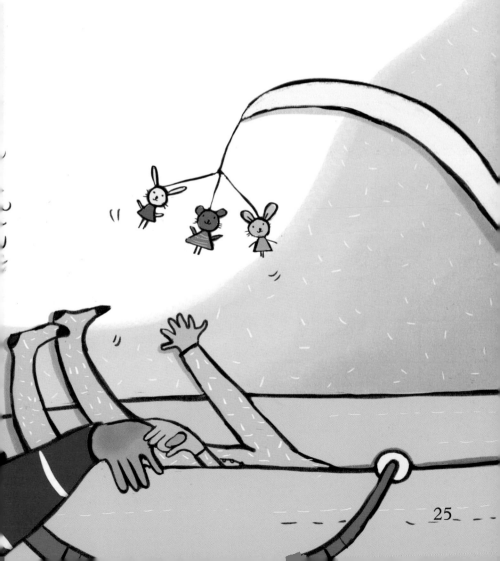

"Shall I read it to you?" Adam asked Mo.
"Eeeeh!" said Mo.
"OK," Adam said.
And he opened the first page.

Chapter Five

"Once there was a…"
Adam read Mo his new book. It was not
as easy as his last book. Some of the
words were hard so he skipped them.

Mo didn't mind. When he had
finished, Adam went back and slowly
read the hard words.
Mo was quiet. She didn't correct him,
like Mum did. She just listened.
Adam read the hard words carefully,
one by one.

"I did it! Thanks, Mo!" he cried.
"Eeeeh!" squealed Mo.

Dad came out of the shower. "Are you
two OK?" he asked.
"We're fine," Adam said, holding Mo's
hand again.

Suddenly, Mum woke up. "Oh my! How's Mo?" she asked.

Adam was beside Mo's basket. "She's fine," he said.

"She's not crying!" Mum cried. "Well done, Adam. Let's read your book while she's quiet."

"I read it to Mo," Adam said. "She liked it."

Mum smiled. "Will you read it to me, too?"

"Sure," Adam said.

He sat down beside Mum and opened the book.

"**Waaaaaahhhh!**" cried Mo.